FIELD NOTES

Memo Book

To Bronwen and David, bear spotters —M. R.

For Sam Williams —D. R.

First published in Great Britain in February 2016 by Bloomsbury Publishing Plc
Published in the United States of America in February 2016 by Bloomsbury Children's Books
www.bloomsbury.com

Bloomsbury is a registered trademark of Bloomsbury Publishing Plc

For information about permission to reproduce selections from this book, write to
Permissions, Bloomsbury Children's Books, 1385 Broadway, New York, New York 10018
Bloomsbury books may be purchased for business or promotional use. For information on bulk purchases please contact
Macmillan Corporate and Premium Sales Department at specialmarkets@macmillan.com

Library of Congress Cataloging-in-Publication Data available upon request
ISBN 978-1-68119-026-6 (hardcover)

Art created with pen, ink, colored pencils, and watercolor
Typeset in Filosofia
Book design by Goldy Broad

Printed in China by C & C Offset Printing Co., Ltd., Shenzhen, Guangdong
10 9 8 7 6 5 4 3 2 1

All papers used by Bloomsbury Publishing, Inc., are natural, recyclable products
made from wood grown in well-managed forests. The manufacturing processes conform
to the environmental regulations of the country of origin.

A Beginner's
Guide to

BEAR
SPOTTING

Michelle
Robinson

illustrated by
David Roberts

BLOOMSBURY
NEW YORK LONDON OXFORD NEW DELHI SYDNEY

Going for a walk in BEAR country?

You'd better make sure you know your bears.

This is a **black** bear.

[Fig. 1. Black Bear, *Ursus americanus*]

This is a **brown** bear.

[FIG. 2. BROWN BEAR, *URSUS ARCTOS*]

And
that is . . .

. . . just plain SILLY.

I don't think you're taking this very seriously.
You ought to, you know.

Bears can be VERY dangerous.

If you get them mixed up, either one of them could **eat** you.

NOW are you paying attention?

Okay, here's what you need to know
before you start walking:

Black bears
are dangerous
and BLACK.

Brown bears
are dangerous
and BROWN.

Although sometimes **brown** bears can be a little BLACK . . .

. . . and **black** bears can be a little BROWN.

Don't worry.
Chances are you won't
even SEE a bear.

Oh, you LUCKY thing!

I think it's a **black** one.

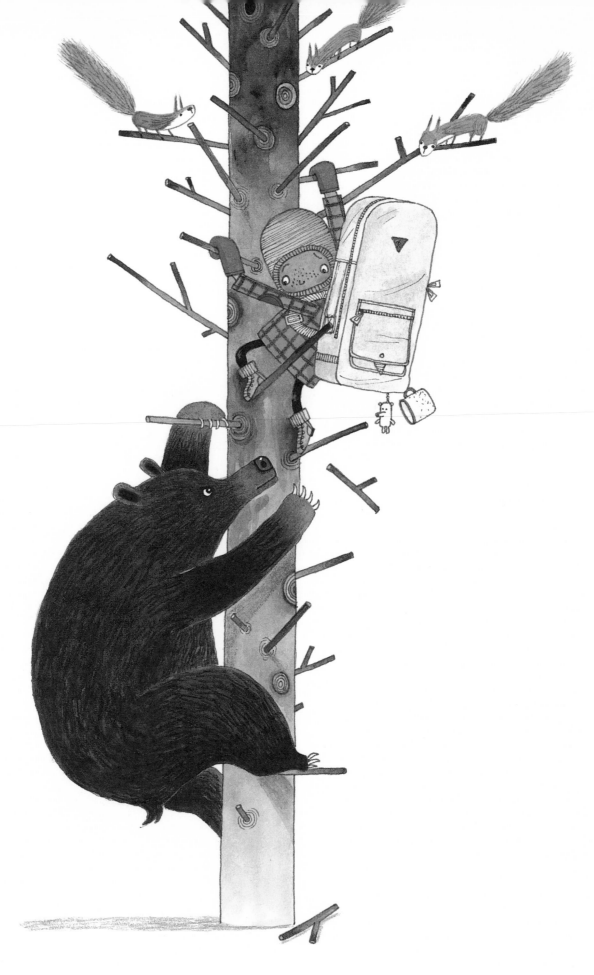

It MUST be.

Brown ones CAN'T climb trees.

Did you know **black** bears weigh about 400 pounds?

With a **black** bear, the

best thing to do is back away *s l o w l y.*

This must
be your
LUCKY
DAY.

You've found a **brown** bear too!

With a **brown** bear, the best thing to do is **play** dead.

Although to a **black** bear, that's like an **invitation** to **dinner**.

This would be a good time
to use your pepper spray.

Pepper spray works on BOTH kinds of bears.

It makes them
d_izzy.

Or was it hungry?

Yep, DEFINITELY hungry.

Got any porridge?

GUM?!

What on earth are you going to do
with a pack of **gum**?

POP!

Of course.
Why didn't I think of that?

Quick!
Run for it!

Oops!

Well, I'm afraid I'm all out of ideas.
Got anything *else* in that bag?

Nope.

Too FLASHY.

That'll
NEVER do.

What did I tell you about
that silly thing?

It's soft and it's silly and it's . . .

. . .WONDERFUL!

It's working!

Well, I never. I take it all back!

Bears *can* be dangerous . . .

. . . but they can also be
very, *very* sweet.

Psst!

Don't forget the **golden rule** of BEAR SPOTTING:

Real bears aren't this friendly.
You should only EVER snuggle up to the **stuffed** kind.

Don't say I didn't warn you.